Whales

Heather Rising

AF605686

Contents

What Are Whales?

Whales are mammals that live in the oceans. Like other mammals, whales are warm-blooded, breathe air and feed their babies with milk.

a humpback whale

All mammals have fur or hair. Baby whales have some hair when they are born. They lose most of it shortly after birth. Adult whales have a few hairs, usually around their mouths and **blowholes**.

There are two main groups of whales – toothed and baleen.

Toothed whales use their teeth to eat fish, squid and even sharks.

Orcas are whales that use their teeth to eat.

The narwhal is a whale with a three-metre tooth, called a tusk, which it uses to spear food.

Baleen whales have **bristles** that hang down from the roof of their mouth. The bristles are called baleen. Baleen is made of keratin. This is the same thing that our own hair and nails are made of.

When water passes through a baleen whale's mouth, **krill** and **plankton** are collected in the baleen. Blue whales can take in over 5000 kilograms of krill a day. That is about the same weight as five small cars.

A grey whale uses its baleen to collect krill and plankton.

Whales have a smooth body with a tail and fins that help them to move through the water. Under their skin, whales have a layer of fat called **blubber**. This fat layer helps the whale to float. It also stops the whale's body heat from escaping, especially in cold water.

Whales store energy in their blubber. Mother whales use this energy when they are feeding milk to their babies.

A mother humpback whale and her baby move through the water together.

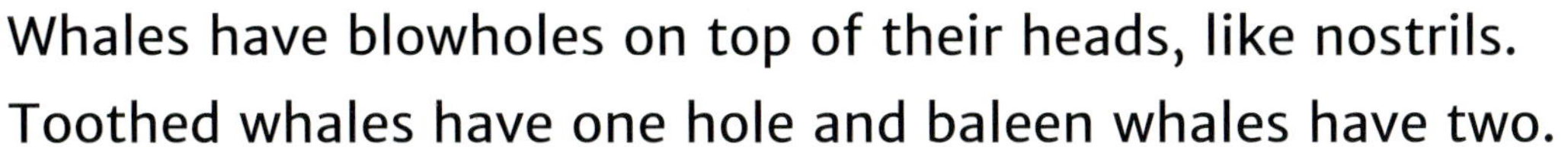

Whales have blowholes on top of their heads, like nostrils. Toothed whales have one hole and baleen whales have two.

When whales come to the surface, they first blow through the blowhole to clear any water. This can shoot a fountain of water or mist into the air. When the water is cleared, whales breathe air through these holes.

A humpback whale shoots a fountain of water through its blowhole.

Different Kinds of Whales

There are many different kinds of whales.

Blue whales are the largest animals to ever live on Earth. They are found in every ocean and can be as long as a basketball court – about 30 metres. They live for around 80 years.

The humpback whale is smaller than the blue whale, but it can grow as long as a bus – about 14 metres. The humpback whale is found all over the world. It **migrates** a longer distance than any other kind of whale.

A humpback whale jumps out of the water.

a blue whale

The pygmy sperm whale is one of the smallest whales at only about 3 metres long. This whale eats squid and crab, and lives in warm waters. The pygmy sperm whale can release a cloud of dark liquid into the water. This helps it to escape a predator.

A pygmy sperm whale releases dark liquid.

Another small whale is the beluga. It has white skin and no fin on its back, so it can swim easily under sheets of ice. It likes very cold water, but in the winter it must move to warmer areas to avoid being trapped by ice. Beluga whales can also live in freshwater rivers.

beluga whales

Where Whales Live

Whales are found in all the world's oceans. They live in groups called **pods**. Pods can be two to three close family members, or as many as 30.

Whales migrate together in pods.

Most whales migrate, or move from one place to another, to feed or give birth. Whales often feed in cold waters around the North **Pole** in the Arctic and the South Pole in Antarctica. They stay there until they have built up a thick layer of blubber. Then they migrate from the poles to warmer water near the **equator** to have their babies.

Humpback Whale Migration

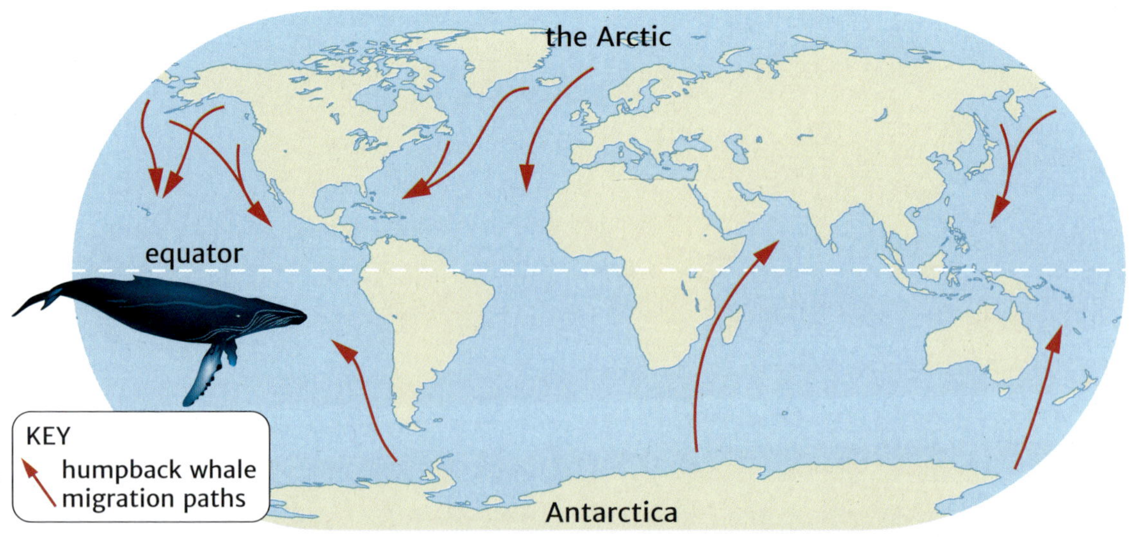

Baby whales are called calves. Calves are born underwater and their mother helps them up to the surface for their first breath.

Calves drink their mother's milk for many months.
The calves do not suck the milk.
Instead, the mother whale squirts it in or near to the calf's mouth.

A calf drinks its mother's milk.

Some whales must dive to find food. Krill is found about 500 metres deep, but other food can be even deeper. Some whales dive as deep as 2000 metres.

Most deep dives by whales are around 1000 metres. That is a distance more than twice around a running track. To reach these depths, whales must hold their breath for a long time – sometimes for more than an hour.

The Cuvier's beaked whale holds the record for the longest dive. One was recorded holding its breath for 138 minutes.

A large pod of sperm whales begin a dive deep into the ocean together.

Whales use clicks, whistles, moans, squeaks and screams to share information with each other. Some of the sounds are very loud – like a rocket taking off. Calves make sounds to their mothers that can be as quiet as a whisper.

Some sounds that whales make are too low for human ears to hear.

When whales repeat sounds or make them in a pattern, they are called "songs".

Three beluga whales use their song to communicate underwater.

Living Alongside Whales

Humans have hunted whales for food for thousands of years. Before electricity, whale oil was used to light lanterns. Baleen was used in hoops for skirts and hats. Ivory from whales was made into art, jewellery and piano keys. Whale products were worth a lot of money.

With powerful ships, whalers could sail in deep water and bring home many whales at once.

This photo from the 1890s shows a ship and a whale that has been caught with a net.

Scientists believe that 90 per cent of the blue whale population was caught and killed by whalers. Many other kinds of whales were also hunted to near **extinction**.

Today, most countries have worked together to stop nearly all whale hunting. The numbers of whales are starting to grow.

Scientists think that about three million whales were killed by humans in the twentieth century.

two blue whales seen from above

Today, some **Indigenous peoples**, such as the Inuit (say: *In-yoo-it*) people in Canada, still hunt whales for food. They do not hunt whales to make money, and when they catch a whale they share it with their whole community. They also watch out for the health of whales in their area.

The Inuit people in Canada hunt whales for food, and share it with their community.

Some Indigenous peoples have stopped hunting whales, and take people whale watching instead. Whale watching can be a way for people to learn about whales and their environment. Whale watchers can help collect information about whales.

People on a whale watching tour see a humpback whale dive.

Whale numbers are slowly increasing, but whales face new dangers. The world's oceans are becoming warmer because of **climate change**. Whales may not find the food they need in warmer waters.

Fishing nets can trap whales and stop them from reaching the surface for air. Noise pollution from boats can confuse a whale's sense of direction. There are international laws to keep boats away from whales, but sometimes whales are still hit by large ships.

This person is rescuing a sperm whale stuck in a fishing net.

Whales can eat floating plastic by mistake.
Plastic rubbish fills their stomachs.
They no longer have any room for food
and they slowly starve.

A whale, or even an entire pod of whales, can become stuck in shallow water or on land. People try to help them by keeping them wet until the tide returns and the whales can swim back out to sea.

People try to help a stranded pod of pilot whales.

One whale washed up on a beach with 40 kilograms of plastic bags in its stomach.

Studying Whales

Scientists want to understand whales better so they can protect them. They use **satellites** to track whale migration paths. The information from the satellites can help ships to avoid whales.

Some scientists put **sensors** on whales to find out how deep they dive. Scientists can learn how far a whale must go to find food.

Scientists study whales in the wild.

Scientists also study the skin, bones and insides of dead whales. They can learn about how the whale died and how healthy it was when alive.

Scientists want to understand more about whale songs. They record the whales and try to understand what information whales are sharing with each other.

Some whale songs are 30 minutes long and are repeated over and over again, for many hours.

People can use a device like this one to listen to the sounds whales make underwater.

We can each do some simple things to protect whales. Reducing our plastic use, and recycling the plastic we do use, is an easy step.

Plastic bags often blow into rivers and waterways and get washed out to sea. Picking them up before they blow away is another way to help whales.

Whales are very important to our oceans.

a humpback whale and its calf

Glossary

blowholes (*noun*) holes on the tops of whales' heads that are used to blow out water and breathe in air

blubber (*noun*) a layer of fat under the skin of marine mammals

bristles (*noun*) short, stiff hairs

climate change (*noun*) a change in weather patterns around the world

equator (*noun*) an imaginary line around the middle of Earth, dividing it into two equal halves

extinction (*noun*) the loss of a type of animal forever

Indigenous peoples (*proper noun*) the first peoples living in an area

krill (*noun*) tiny animals with shells that live in the sea

migrates (*verb*) moves from one place to another

plankton (*noun*) very tiny living creatures found in water

pods (*noun*) groups of marine animals, such as whales or dolphins

pole (*noun*) one of the two opposite points on Earth around which the planet turns

satellites (*noun*) objects sent into space to orbit around a planet

sensors (*noun*) devices used to measure things like depth, temperature or light

Index